Colin

AL and TEDDY

Dear Lovers of Books and Children,

I'd like to take this opportunity to introduce you to Dream Yard Press,

a creation of Dream Yard Project, the largest provider of the arts

to the children of the Bronx. Proceeds from the sales of Al and Teddy

will be used to purchase computers, pencils, sketch pads,

journals, oil paints, and pizza.

It is our hope that you'll join us and help support our kids.

NW

AL and TEDDY

story and illustrations by
Neil Waldman

Dream Yard Press

Published by Dream Yard Press

1085 Washington Avenue

Bronx, New York 10456

Waldman, Neil

Al and Teddy / Neil Waldman

FIRST EDITION

10 9 8 7 6 5 4 3 2 1

Printed in Malaysia

For the young painters,

poets, dancers and dreamers

of the Bronx

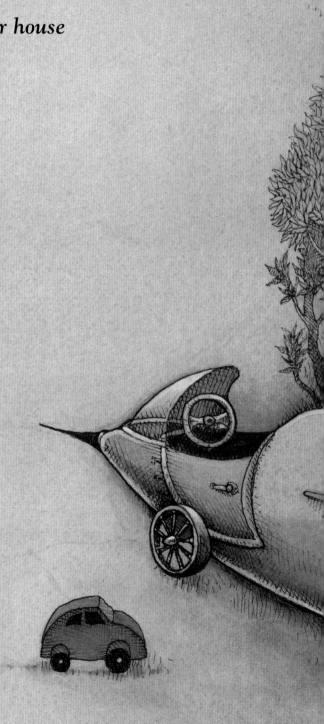

When everyone is sleeping

and Saturn circles in the midnight sky,

my big brother Al tiptoes out of our house

and flies to places faraway.

But when I asked if I could come,
he'd shake his head and say,
"Sorry, Teddy.

"Maybe in a year or two

you'll be big enough

to fly with me.

"I'll see you in the morning."

And when the morning sun started

slipping through my window,

I'd climb out of bed

and head for Al's room

. . . and he was always there!

"Hey, who's that?" I asked him.

"It's me, of course," Al answered,

"sailing to my kingdom."

"Your kingdom?

How can you have a kingdom?

You're only seven!"

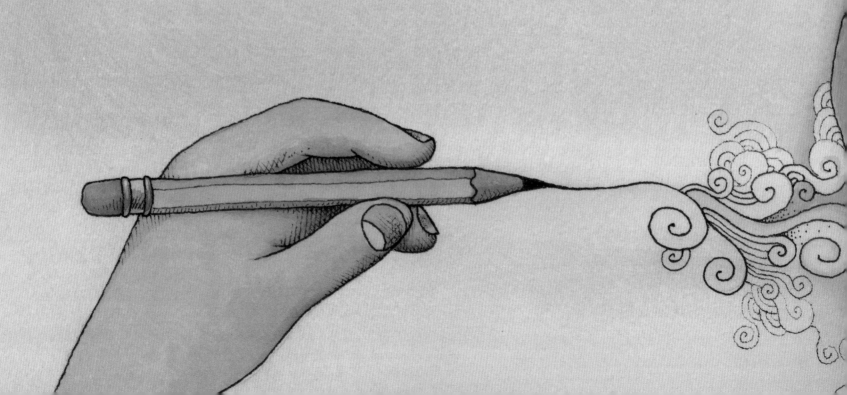

"I'm not really seven!" Al said.

"What do you mean, you're not really seven?"

"Do you know what my name is?"

"Sure! It's Big Al!"

"That's not my real name," he said.

"Then what is your real name?"

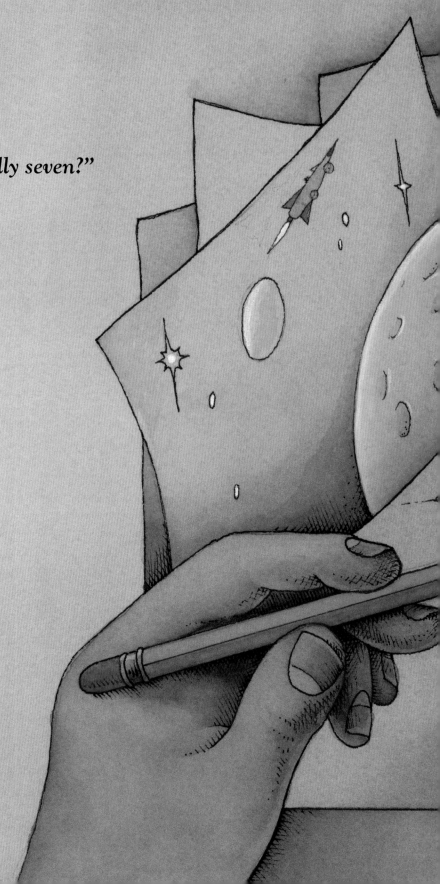

"King Alejandro."

"So now you're telling me you're a king?"

"Yep — with my own private castle

and my very own stallion

and there's a pony named Snowflake

waiting for you, Teddy."

"For ME?"

"Yep. You're going to be called Prince Teodoro."

"Holy cow!" I said. "Lets go now!"

"Sorry, Teddy. There are rules in my kingdom

and one of them says no one gets in till he's five."

"BUT I'M ONLY FOUR!"

I stormed out of Big Al's room,

    but then I remembered Snowflake

    and when I got back

    I was smiling.

"I can wait!" I said,

"and Al . . . could you make me

    one more picture?"

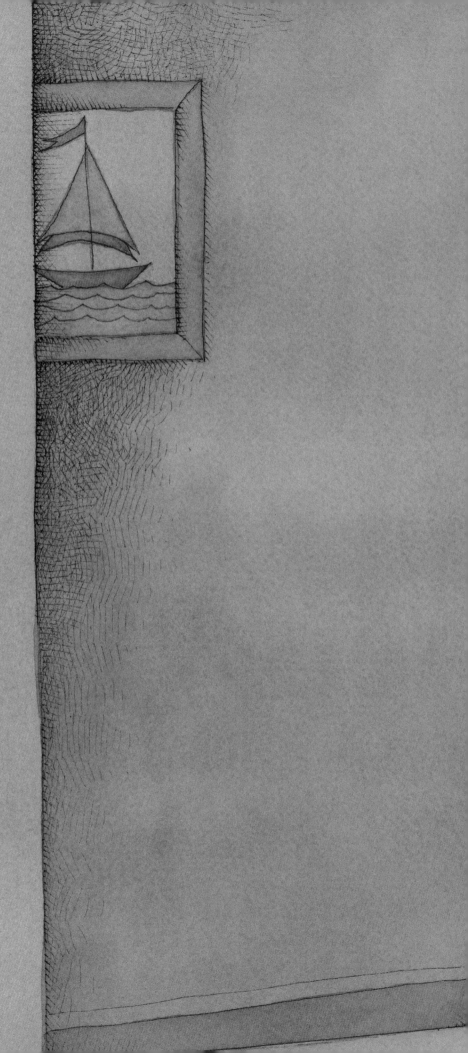

"Hey, who's that?" I asked.

"It's the moon monster, of course," Al answered.
"I shot him with my paintbrush
and turned him into a picture."

"Holy cow!" I said.

Then I sped past seconds

and millions of minutes

until I turned five.

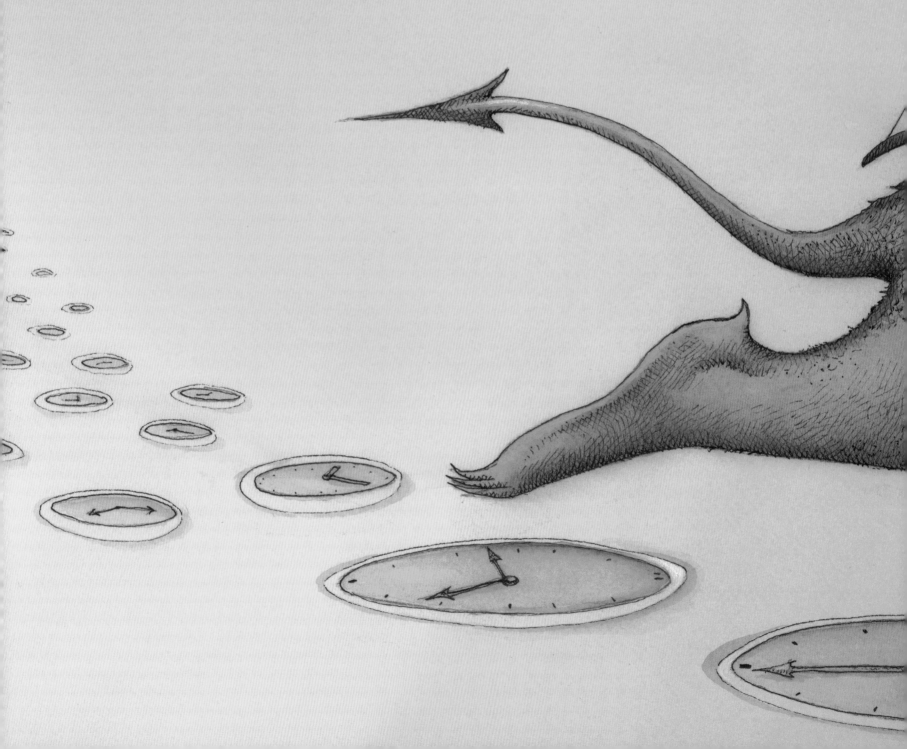

"Hey, Al! Time to go!"

"Not yet, Teddy. They just changed one of the rules.
    You have to be six to get in."

"YOU KNOW I'M NOT SIX
    . . . and if you won't take me now
        everybody's gonna know
            you're nothing but a BIG FAT LIAR!"

"Please don't say that, Teddy.

It was just so cool making up those stories,

and anyway, Teddy . . . are you gonna hate me

for the rest of your life?"

"I REALLY WANTED THAT PONY!" I yelled.

"But I could never hate you.

You're my big brother.

I love you more than any old horse!

Could you make me one more picture?"

Al went over to his desk, took out two pencils
and handed one to me.

"So Prince Teodoro," he said,

with a smile as big as Saturn,

"wanna fly?"

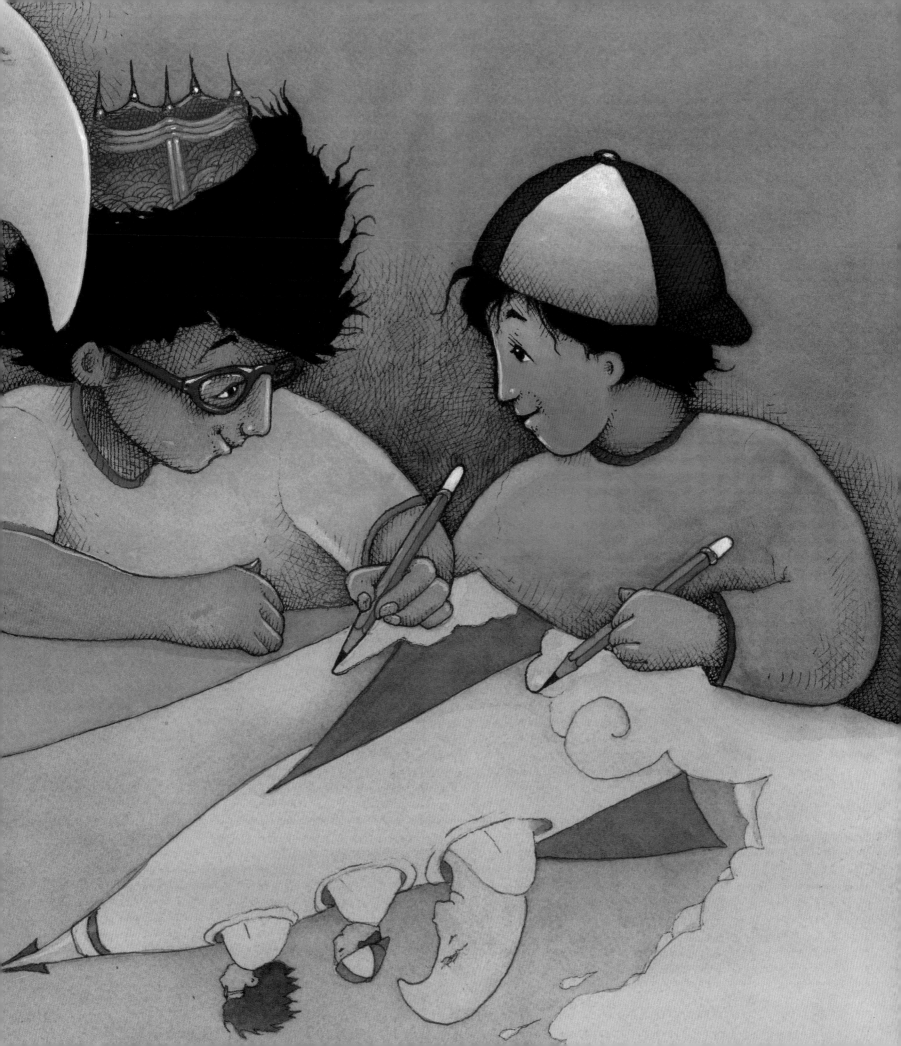

THANKS

to Maurice Sendak
whose support, encouragement, and genius
have been my beacon

to Judy O'Malley, whose keen eye
illuminated the music
of Al and Teddy's voices

to Stephen Roxburgh, who helped me
to uncover the core
of the manuscript

and to Barbara Aronica-Buck,
who sculpted the typographic forms
that grace every page